Jack and Jill

Jack and Jill went up the hill
To fetch a pail of water;
Jack fell down and broke his crown,
and Jill came tumbling after.

Rub-a-Dub-Dub

Rub-a-dub-dub,
Three men in a tub,
And who do you think they be?
The butcher, the baker,
The candlestick-maker,
All put out to sea.

Old King Cole

Old King Cole
Was a merry old soul,
And a merry old soul was he;
He called for his pipe,
And he called for his bowl,
And he called for his fiddlers three!

Wee Willie Winkie

Wee Willie Winkie runs through the town,
Upstairs and downstairs, in his nightgown;
Rapping at the window, crying through the lock,
"Are the children in their beds?
Now it's eight o'clock."

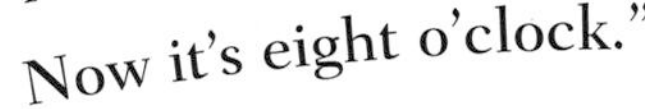

GIRLS AND BOYS COME OUT TO PLAY

Illustrated by
Tracey Campbell Pearson

MARGARET FERGUSON BOOKS
HOLIDAY HOUSE • NEW YORK

MOTHER GOOSE

Margaret Ferguson Books

HOLIDAY HOUSE is registered in the U.S. Patent and Trademark Office.
Printed and bound in December 2020 at Leo Paper, Heshan, China.
The artwork was created with pen and ink and watercolor on Fabriano paper.
www.holidayhouse.com
First Edition
1 3 5 7 9 10 8 6 4 2

Library of Congress Cataloging-in-Publication Data
Names: Pearson, Tracey Campbell, illustrator.
Title: Girls and boys come out to play / illustrated by Tracey Campbell Pearson.
Description: New York City : Holiday House, 2021. | "Margaret Ferguson Books."
Audience: Ages 4–6. | Audience: Grades K–1. | Summary: "Mother Goose invites children on a city block to come out and play and when they do, they meet some of her most famous nursery rhyme characters"—Provided by publisher.
Identifiers: LCCN 2019055105 | ISBN 9780823447138 (hardcover)
Subjects: LCSH: Nursery rhymes. | Children's poetry. | CYAC: Nursery rhymes.
Classification: LCC PZ8.3.P2748 Gir 2021 | DDC 398.8—dc23
LC record available at https://lccn.loc.gov/2019055105
ISBN: 978-0-8234-4713-8 (hardcover)

The Cow

The Baker
The Cat
Humpty Dumpty
Mother Goose

Girls and boys come out to play,

The moon doth shine as bright as day.

MOTHER GOOSE

Leave your supper,

Leave your sleep,

And come with your playfellows into the street.

Come with a whoop, come with a call,

Come with good will . . . or not at all.

Up the ladder . . .

. . . and down the wall.

A halfpenny roll will serve us all.

B.B.&C

You find the milk . . .

and I'll find the flour.

And we'll have pudding in half an hour.

BB&C
FLOUR

BB&C

MOTHER GOOSE

MOTHER
GOOSE

Good night.
Sweet dreams.

Hey, Diddle, Diddle

Hey, diddle, diddle,
The cat and the fiddle,
The cow jumped over the moon;
The little dog laughed
To see such sport,
And the dish ran away with the spoon.

Ring Around the Rosy

Ring around the rosy,
Pocket full of posy,
Ashes! Ashes!
We all fall down!

Humpty Dumpty

Humpty Dumpty sat on a wall,
Humpty Dumpty had a great fall;
All the king's horses and all the king's men
Couldn't put Humpty together again.

Little Boy Blue

Little boy blue,
Come blow your horn,
The sheep's in the meadow,
The cow's in the corn.
But where is the boy
Who looks after the sheep?
He's under a haystack,
Fast asleep.